Just as Happy

To Mira,
Don Hansbrough

Fairy Tales

Don Hansbrough

Just as Happy

Fairy Tales

Don Hansbrough

In these tales,

you may see,

farther than

a fairy's dream.

The author may be

far away,

perhaps beyond

the stars this day.

Yet, a part

of him remains,

in the whisper of

each turning page.

The Littlest Dragon

The Littlest Dragon chased the very naughty stars.

It was his turn to light them.

They just would not let him!

"From Pearl Moon to Morning Sun, you shall never catch us, Littlest Dragon!"

Then, the littlest child in the World sang an evening song. It was so beautiful, all the stars stopped to listen.

The Littlest Dragon lit them.

Morning Sun and Star

The last star asked the Morning Sun, "How did you become so big and bright?"

The Sun replied, "While other stars chose to shine on some, I chose to shine on everyone."

The last star chose to follow such a wise teacher, and became the Morning Star.

The Evil Giant and Tiny Wren

An evil giant came to the land. He stole many cows and hens. He ate crops.

He was especially fond of strawberries.

His mighty arms destroyed villages. His careless footsteps wrecked woodlands. Even the Emperor's fairy soldiers were no match for him.

No one knew what to do.

Then, a tiny bird had an idea. She was just a common wren, but kind and wise.

Every evening, she left her warm, safe nest. She flew to the valley where the giant slept. There, she sang all night, keeping him awake. Her dull color and smallness kept the giant from finding where she hid.

Many nights passed. The giant, tired and weeping, left the land.

He would never eat strawberries again.

Now the Dragon King watched all this. He was most impressed. Appearing with his many dragon followers, he roared, "Tiny wren! Sit beside me forever, on my jeweled throne in the heavens!"

"No thank you." replied the tiny wren. "I prefer to remain in my own simple nest, sharing songs with the farmers' children."

The Caterpillar

The caterpillar climbed the sky, to see the lovely butterflies.

Oh, how he loved them!

Oh, how he adored them!

"If only I could be so fine!" he cried, climbing the ivy vine. Then, up the oak he went.

"You are just as fine!" a soft voice said. "You simply do not know it yet!"

It was a butterfly who spoke, a part of the kaleidoscope, of jolly friends lit by the Sun.

The caterpillar did not know. In his cocoon, he wept and slept.

He simply did not know it yet.

Yet, every butterfly remembers, struggling as a caterpillar. It is a happy memory, filled with hopes and dreams.

The Sweet Peach

The Sweet Peach was left outside the Monkey Palace, by a sleepy child.

"Come live with us!" squeaked the Monkey King. "We would never eat you, for our fine chef feeds us very well. You shall be an honorary monkey!"

So the Sweet Peach rolled into the Monkey Palace, soon becoming very, very fuzzy, It began to believe it was a monkey.

One morning, their fine chef was late with breakfast.

The Sweet Peach was eaten.

Cats Spat

Cats spat all through the night.

They argued over silly things, things only cats can understand.

They woke babies from their dreams. Babies cried, waking everything.

Still, the Golden Moon was not disturbed, as it rose to comfort the stars.

The Stained Glass Angel

The stained glass angel lived in a window, at the top of the cathedral.

She was named Violette by young apprentice, Jean. His generous master allowed him to fashion one small angel. Jean had many skills to learn, so Violette was rather crude. No one noticed, she was so high up.

No one noticed, except the gargoyles. They loved to snap their stone tails and wail, "You are ugly and not a real angel!"

One gargoyle refused to taunt. Songbirds nested on his shoulders. He let their music speak for him.

Though cruel words made her shed a tear, Violette knew in her heart she was more than lead and glass. She was the dawn light sent from above, to touch the sweetest, kindest child. At night, when the cathedral candles glowed, her light returned to the heavens.

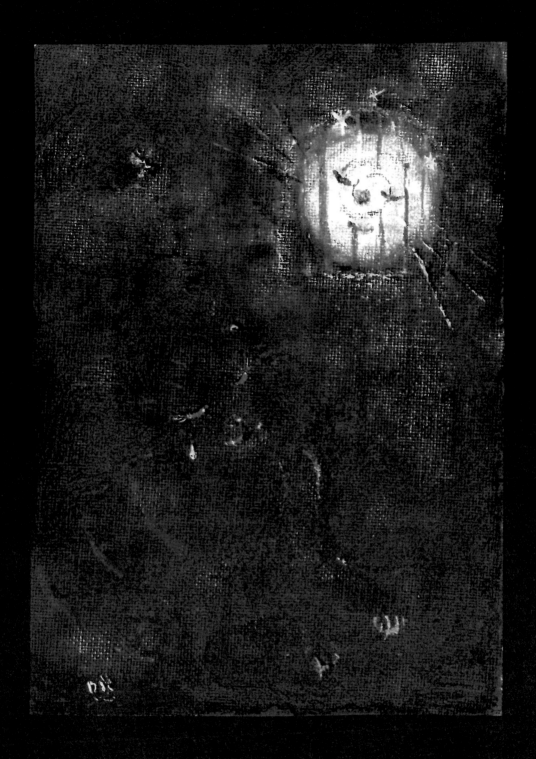

The Tiger Moon

The lonely tiger in the zoo, greeted his friend, the Golden Moon, with a roar, then a purr, above the snores of all the creatures in their rooms.

Peeking through the dark bars of his den, the Moon became a tiger friend.

The Magic Folding Screen

Over the mountains, in a deep forest, a humble artist lived.

He painted a folding screen, so beautiful, naughty wood fairies peeking in the window of his hut, shed magic tears upon it.

The folding screen was his gift to the Emperor's daughter, soon to wed a prince across the sea. The Princess received many lovely gifts. She made sure to thank everyone, except the humble artist. His gift was deemed unworthy, for when he carried it over the mountains, the frame was dented and cracked.

How unfortunate! Within, he had painted a most strange, but wondrous land.

It was a land of pink and silver palaces, of brilliant gardens and deep emerald forests, where the gentlest creatures chose to gather. Above this land, an even lovelier world floated, home to winged and saintly beings. I am told, anyone gazing into this world, eventually finds himself up there. Of course, it takes some patience to do this.

The folding screen was simply tossed into the royal ship's hold, as the Princess sailed off to her new life.

Now, the voyage began with sunny days and starry nights, when dolphins sang sweet lullabies.

One night, the dolphins did not sing. There was a great storm.

It was a storm to shame other storms. The royal ship was tossed and broken into a thousand royal pieces. The Princess found herself all alone in the world. A large piece of wreckage was all that kept her from perishing.

It was the beautiful folding screen.

Her fingers fitted perfectly into the dents and scratches. The folding screen became her boat, carrying her to a most strange, but wondrous land.

It was a land of pink and silver palaces, of brilliant gardens and deep emerald forests, where the gentlest creatures chose to gather. Above this land and even lovelier world floated, home to winged and saintly beings. I am told, anyone gazing into this world, eventually finds oneself up there. Of course, it takes some patience to do this.

There, the Princess married a kind, young man, far nobler than the one arranged for her. There was a grand celebration, and the happy couple received may lovely gifts.

However, no gift compared to the beautiful folding screen, she had never said thank you for.

This was her only sorrow.

The Mirror Girl

A most unusual child was born.

She was a mirror, as well as a child.

Mother and Father were quite upset, until they saw the beauty of it. At night, she reflected all the stars. This hid their child from any harm. In summer, their garden flowers bloomed biggest and brightest from the extra sun.

Of course, the vain always admired her, just to admire their own reflections. Others often argued, claiming, "She only looks like us!"

Those who were true friends, simply did not care. They loved her. She loved them. Even when they were very sad, her smile embraced each face.

Lovely Emily

Lovely Emily loved to paint fairies. This was difficult to do, to paint such tiny beings, in tiny fairy lands.

One day she thought, "I will paint them bigger!" The fairies grew in every painting, until they were the size of her.

Then, Emily became a fairy.

Some say the fairies did not grow, that Emily grew smaller and smaller.

Surely it does not really matter, in this wonderful, magical world.

The Bamboo Flute

The bamboo flute lived in the forest, with many bamboo friends.

"I am happy!" it whispered.

One morning, it was chopped down and carried away.

"I am so sad!"

The tree was carved into a flute, sharing songs the pandas dream.

"I am happy once again!"

Then, the sweet young man who played it, lost his flute friend in a storm.

"I have never been so sad!"

Slowly, slowly, the forest grew, around the spot the flute was lost.

The bamboo flute was home again, with many bamboo friends.

There Once was a World

There once was a world, where cruel words made one uglier, where kind words made one lovelier.

Yet, no one knew this, for in this world, every single soul was blind.

Only the flowers were gifted with sight, and their only language is love.

Especially Delicious

The early flowers gathered round, The Great, The Wise, All-Seeing One. He appeared on the beautiful, blue stone, where field and woodland meet.

The meadow mice soon joined their friends, for all mice are seekers of wisdom.

Sadly, the fellow turned out to be, just a slightly old potato, beginning to grow eyes.

Yet, it had been a long and hungry winter, making The Great, The Wise, All-Seeing One, especially delicious.

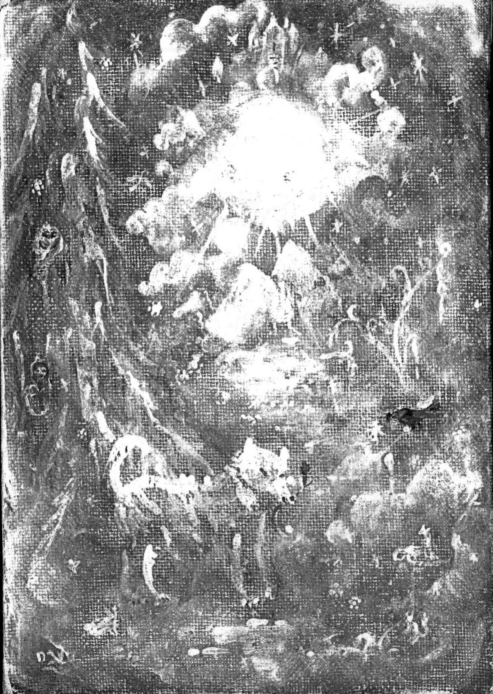

The Especially Good Wolf

There once was a good wolf.

Yes, all wolves are good. This one was especially kind and gentle. He not only cared about the little creatures in his woods. He cared about the ones in other woods as well.

The villagers believed the wolf was bad. When they saw him, they threw stones. The little children would throw pebbles, except one new girl named Lavender, living with her grandfather.

Lavender came from a warm land without winter, so on the first snowy day, she was the first child to run out to play. She was drawn to the woods. It had become a frosty, wild cathedral. Delicate icicles hung from the trees, painting everything in stained glass rainbows. There was heavenly music, for Sir Robin, daring to remain all winter, was also very pleased.

Lavender wandered in this wonder, deep into the woods, past time for supper. She became lost, yet she was not lost, for the gentle wolf was watching her. He led her back to her grandfather's den we humans call a home.

There, the villagers still threw their stones. Though the little children threw their pebbles, as the gentle wolf had watched Lavender, the Queen of All Fairies watched the wolf.

She appeared with her many fairy children. They held falling star torches and rode green-eyed kittens. They led the wolf back to his woods, then over the mountains to his dear mother's den.

For great goodness draws great goodness to it. She was the one who taught him to be especially kind and gentle.

The Dragonfly

The dragonfly sat on the stone.

The stone sat in the mighty river.

A tiny daisy kept him company.

Though hungry carp wished he was their dinner, he was very safe.

The dragonfly was a simple creature. He did not know where he had flown from, or where he would be flying to.

The bright Sun warmed his golden wings.

How happy he was, to simply know, he made the world more beautiful.

I Dreamed I Rode a Unicorn

I dreamed I rode a unicorn,
through sunless kingdoms, so forlorn,

where every spot we stopped awhile,
grew flowers, blooming children's smiles.

Then, morning came. When I awoke,
as dawn birds sang, my own heart spoke,

perhaps, a unicorn had dreamed,
that I was real and riding him.

Just as Happy

A wise sage once said, "When one lives in a palace for too long, one no longer notices the sweet perfume."

This was true for the Prince. He lived in a golden palace, embraced by lilac gardens. He was also fair of face. He had his choice of royal or common mate.

Yet, the Prince was unhappy. He could not see his great fortune, having lived with it all his life.

Others could see it. How they envied him! That is, except for one young man, so poor, he lived beneath a tree. Yet, he was very happy.

His rooftop cradled the songs of birds, offering his wishing star a special perch. There, he watched the glorious Sun rise and set on all the kingdoms in the world, filled with countless friends.

Friends filled with countless hopes and dreams. To his star he wished, they would all become just as happy.

The Little Book

In a dark corner of a great and ancient library, a little book of fairy tales, began to grow arms and legs.

No one noticed, for it was a very dusty book, in a most hidden corner.

At first, the arms and legs were simply broken threads of binding. Working together, they grew and lengthened. Hearing this, the snoring words awoke from their dreams. They were quite inspired to become, a beautiful head and heart.

Years past. The dear little book became a real and complete person. Indeed, it became the author himself.

Yet, no one in the library noticed this, for as the fairy tale book became the author, they had all become books.

Made in the USA
San Bernardino, CA
15 June 2018